Sir Prickles
The Hedgehog Knight

Chantal Goldenberg

$9.95 Can

LIBRARY AND ARCHIVES CANADA CATALOGUING IN PUBLICATION

Goldenberg, Chantal, 1975-, author, illustrator
Sir Prickles the hedgehog knight / Chantal Goldenberg.
ISBN 978-0-9936881-2-6 (pbk.)
I. Title
PS8613.O4395S57 2014   jC813'.6   C2014-901322-1

Copyright © 2014 Chantal Goldenberg

All rights reserved. Except for use in any review or critical article, the reproduction or use of this work, in whole or in part, in any form by any electronic, mechanical or other means—including xerography, photocopying and recording—or in any information or storage retrieval system, is forbidden without express permission of the publisher

Published by
LOOSE CANNON PRESS

Chantal Goldenberg

Sir Prickles the Hedgehog Knight

In the time of Camelot and King Arthur, there happened many strange and wonderful things. And perhaps the strangest and most wonderful story is not about a man (though there were many great men), or a lady (though there were many great ladies), but about a hedgehog. And he was the greatest hero of them all.

His name was Prickles, and even as a very young hedge-piggie, all he ever wanted to be was a knight. And not just any knight, but a knight of the Round Table. All his heroes were knights: Sir Gawaine, Sir Galahad, and the great Sir Lancelot himself. People everywhere had heard the stories, and told them to each other. Was it such a surprise that the animals listened, too?

Everyone loved King Arthur, because they knew that he loved them. He was kind and wise, and known to deal fairly with both man and beast. Still, it was Lancelot that was Prickles' special favourite. Brave Sir Lancelot, who fought

Chantal Goldenberg

ogres and giants, rescued damsels in distress, and even tried to find a dragon to fight, though he hadn't found one yet. Oh, how Prickles dreamed of fighting by his side, and what wonderful friends they would be!

The other animals all laughed at him. Even his family were concerned. His father said, "You're just a silly little hedgehog. You're too small to be a knight. Do something useful, like digging a burrow."

His mother said, "It's so dangerous to be a knight. You're my sweet little hedgehog. Stay home and help me gather food for winter."

But Prickles didn't care that he was just a hedgehog. He was going to be a knight. So when he was old enough, he kissed his mother and father goodbye, and waddled off to King Arthur's court. What a long, long way it was, and what a very big castle! Camelot was bigger than anything he had ever seen, and he almost turned back then.

That's when it happened. Sir Lancelot crossed the hall right in front of him! Prickles couldn't believe his luck. He scurried after his hero, his claws clicking and clacking over the slippery marble floor.

Huffing and puffing to keep up, the poor little hedgehog was barely paying attention to where he was going, and smack! He ran right into a table leg. But not just any table leg. As he looked up, and up, and up, Prickles saw that he had followed his hero straight to the Round Table!

They were all there. Sir Lancelot, of course, just sitting down, and beside him were Sir Gawaine and Sir Galahad, and all the others. And there, just on Lancelot's other side, the side that Prickles just happened to have crashed into, was the king.

"What's this?" came a voice, booming from above. "Are we having the forest in for tea, now?"

It was another knight, Sir Wyeth, who was large and smelly. He grinned a grin full of teeth, and scooped little Prickles up. "Our guest is too small to sit at the table, but too dirty to sit on it!"

The rest of the knights roared with laughter.

"Please, sir," said Prickles, quite upset by this, "I am small, this is true. But I assure you I am quite clean, and to say otherwise is an insult to my honour. I must ask you to apologize."

The others thought this was even funnier, but Wyeth was no longer laughing. "Why, you puny little hedgehog… Ow!"

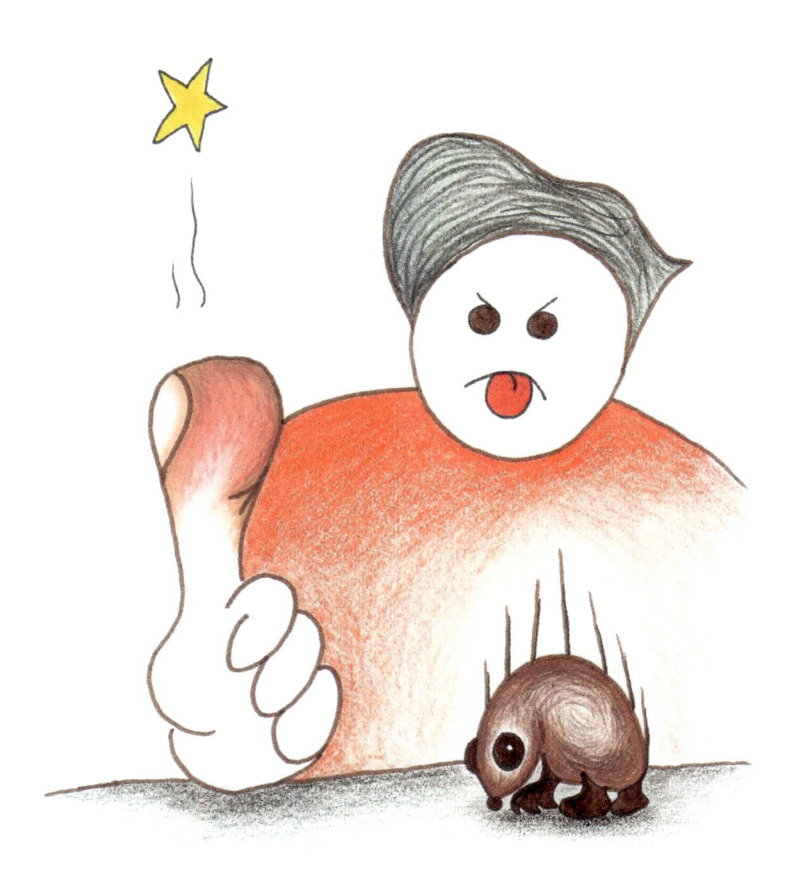

And he dropped Prickles onto the table so he could suck his thumb, which had been stuck by one of the hedgehog's short quills.

When they saw this, the knights couldn't contain themselves, and laughed till they cried. But they stopped laughing when Wyeth raised his heavy plate to squash the hedgehog.

"Enough!" thundered King Arthur. "I have seen enough. Wyeth, sit, and all you others, hold your tongues."

"But, my lord," Wyeth said, "I demand satisfaction. That creature insulted me."

The king was very stern. "From what I saw, it was you who insulted him. You refused him satisfaction, and were taught a lesson I had thought all my knights knew: to be polite and chivalrous to all, whoever they may be."

Wyeth sat, still sulking.

"Now," the king went on, "what have we here? What is your name, my good fellow?"

Coming a bit closer and standing at attention on his hind legs, the little hedgehog announced, "My name is Prickles, your Majesty. All my life, I have heard of the Knights of the

Round Table, and have longed to be one of them. I beg you, please, to make me a page or a squire to one of these fine gentlemen, so that one day, I too may be a knight."

Here, the laughter started again, and Wyeth laughed loudest. "What? A knight? Impossible! Hedgehogs can't be knights, how could he even use a sword?"

"I beg your pardon, sir," said Prickles, "but I have brought my own sword."

And here he drew out of his fur one very long quill he had grown just for this reason. It was very, very sharp, and Wyeth was suddenly glad his thumb didn't get stuck with that.

Prickles did look a little fiercer holding his special quill. But the knights weren't convinced.

"How will he fight?" asked Sir Lancelot. "He may have a sword, but who will be his teacher? He cannot defend himself."

"Yes," said Sir Galahad, who had a tender heart, "I would not want to be responsible if he were hurt."

"Nor I," said Sir Gawaine.

King Arthur thought a long time before speaking. "There is more to being a knight than fighting and swords. A true knight must have great courage, and be pure of heart. Hedgehog Prickles, would you prove yourself to be such a knight, and worthy to sit at the Round Table?"

"Oh, yes, your Majesty!" Prickles said.

"Then I set you a quest: to rescue a damsel in distress, defeat a dragon, or face your enemy in honourable combat, and become the best of friends. Then we shall know your heart."

Lancelot led everyone in a cheer as Prickles went on his way. "Hip Hip Hooray! Hip Hip Hooray!" The only one who didn't join in was Sir Wyeth, who was sucking his injured thumb again, and not looking too happy about it.

But who cared about him? It was a wonderful, beautiful day, and Prickles was starting off on his very own quest. A quest! Never in his wildest dreams did he imagine he'd be given such a chance. Camelot was far behind him now, and the road was deserted. There was no one else, human or animal, as far as the eye could see. But there was a noise, a strange and desperate noise, and when Prickles got closer he heard what it was.

It was a milkmaid, and three large, smelly men were chasing her. They looked a little like Sir Wyeth. They smelled like him too. "Help, help!" the milkmaid cried. "They're thieves and they stole all my milk!" She found a tree and climbed up while the men laughed below.

Prickles was nearly dancing, he was so excited. This was it! Here was a damsel in distress, and if he could help her, it would fulfill his quest and show King Arthur that he was a true knight, and that his heart was pure.

So he scurried up to the thieves and said, "Stop right there! How dare you? This damsel is in distress, and I'm going to rescue her."

"Whoever heard of a hedgehog knight?" the thieves said.

"Well, actually, I'm not a knight yet," Prickles admitted. "I'm on a quest, and if I can show King Arthur that I'm a true knight, and that I have a pure heart, he'll let me sit at the Round Table."

"A quest!" giggled one thief.

"A pure heart!" guffawed another.

"King Arthur and the Round Table!" roared the last.

And they all fell laughing to the ground.

Sir Prickles, The Hedgehog Knight

"Pssst!" Prickles said to the milkmaid. "You can come down now. Even if I can't rescue you, I can still distract them long enough for you to get away."

She climbed down the tree, and gave him a little kiss. "I hope you fulfill your quest," she said, before she ran home.

Now that the damsel in distress was gone, Prickles gave the thieves the same lesson he had given Sir Wyeth, and left them all sucking their thumbs.

Further down the road, he came to a mountain. And he heard a noise, a strange and desolate noise, and soon he found out what it was.

It was sniffling. Huge, giant, enormous sniffling. In fact the closer he got, the more it sounded like snuffling. And when he found the cave it was coming from, he found out why.

A dragon! A huge, golden dragon, curled tight underground, bigger than Camelot, bigger than the biggest mountain. This was it! No one else had ever found a dragon, not even Sir

Lancelot, and now was Prickles' chance to defeat him. If he did, he would fulfill his quest and show King Arthur that he was a true knight, and that his heart was pure.

But the more he listened, the sadder the dragon sounded. In fact now he started sobbing. This dragon was already defeated.

Prickles felt sorry for him, and came as close as he dared. "Excuse me," he squeaked, then, trying to sound brave, he said, "I couldn't help but hear you crying. Are you all right?"

The dragon looked quickly around. "Who's that?" he said. "Who's there? Answer me, or I'll roast you!"

Now Prickles was very scared, but he forced himself to say, "My name is Prickles. Is there anything wrong?"

The dragon seemed to relax, and sighed, "Oh, good, it's just a hedgehog. I was afraid those horrible thieves had come back."

"What thieves?" said Prickles.

"They were large, smelly humans, and they stole some of my gold scales. They said they were taking them to their brother at Camelot. I tried to stop them, but I don't like to fight. I wouldn't really have roasted you, you know."

"Thank you," said Prickles. "Is there anything I can do to help?"

The dragon started crying again. "I don't think so. You see, those scales were very important to me. Without them, all my golden armour is coming undone, and soon I won't have any left at all."

"Oh, well, that's easy to fix," Prickles said. "I learned how to sew when I was just a wee little hedge-piggie, and I grew my very first quill."

And using his sword like a very large, very strong needle, he sewed the dragon's armour up tight.

"Oh, thank you, Sir Hedgehog!" the dragon said. "You are very kind."

"Glad to help. But I'm not really a knight, not yet anyway. Wish me luck on my quest!"

And with that, Prickles went on his way.

After a time, he came to a run-down farmhouse, and he heard a strange and terrible noise, a yowling, growling, hissing, howling noise. Soon he found out what it was.

It was a cat. At least he thought it was a cat, its fur was so dirty and tangled. It seemed to be very, very angry, running around screeching and shrieking, and Prickles could see its strong white teeth and sharp claws.

At last! This had to be it! This was indeed a worthy foe, and he looked ready for a fight. If Prickles won, he just might impress that cat enough to want to be friends, and he would fulfill his quest. Then King Arthur would surely see that he really was a true knight, with a pure heart.

"Halt!" Prickles said, drawing his sword. "My name is Prickles the Hedgehog, and I challenge thee to a duel!"

The cat did not halt. It came racing straight for him! Prickles fought long and hard, but he only had one long quill against all those teeth and claws. Finally he did the only thing he could. He rolled in a ball and stuck out all his smaller quills.

The cat swiped at him with one furry paw, which quickly got snagged. "Wait a minute," the cat said. "Did you say you were a hedgehog?"

Prickles took a peek at his attacker. "Y-yes…"

The cat was suddenly very excited. "I haven't been brushed in so long! Would you mind, um…"

"Glad to help!" Prickles said, with a very relieved sigh. And using his body like a sort of comb, he ran up and down and all over that cat, until his fur was sleek and glossy and really quite handsome.

"Oh, thank you!" purred the cat. "My name is Whiskers, and that felt so good! My master is hardly ever home, and even when he is, he never brushes me. He's allergic to clean cats. All he does is plan robberies with his three brothers."

"Really?" said Prickles. "What's his name?"

"His name is Sir Wyeth. He is a large and smelly man, and he is a knight of the Round Table."

"Oh no he's not!" Prickles was very angry. "He's only pretending! King Arthur told me that a true knight has a pure heart. And after meeting Sir Wyeth's brothers, and the milkmaid and the dragon, I know I have to go back to

Camelot. I have to warn the king there's a traitor at his table. Whiskers, will you come with me to tell your story?"

Whiskers said, "Yes! Let's go!"

Along the way, they stopped to ask the dragon if he wanted to come. He didn't want to leave his cave, but he gave them a few very small gold scales. Then they went to the milkmaid, but she didn't want to leave her dairy. She gave them some milk to drink, and some cheese to take away with them to Camelot.

When they were once again standing before King Arthur and all his knights, Sir Lancelot said, "So, little hedgehog, you seem to have made a friend. Did you fulfill your quest? Was this friend once a foe?"

Prickles sighed a little. "Not really. It turns out he was just upset. His name is Whiskers, and he has a story to tell."

When Whiskers was done, King Arthur looked very concerned. "I hope you are mistaken about Sir Wyeth, my good cat. Do you have any proof of this story?"

Whiskers brought out the cheese he had been carrying. "This is a gift from the milkmaid that Prickles saved from Sir Wyeth's brothers."

Sir Lancelot turned again to the little hedgehog. "Is this true?" he said. "Did you fulfill your quest and rescue a damsel in distress?"

"Well, not exactly." Prickles pouted a little. "The thieves were laughing too hard to fight them properly."

"But he did manage to distract them," Whiskers piped up. "So the milkmaid could get away."

King Arthur said, "I'm glad she is safe. But spilled milk is nothing to cry about. Did these thieves steal from anyone else?"

"Yes!" said Whiskers. "They ripped golden scales from a dragon."

Here there was an excited whispering. No one had ever found a dragon, not even Sir Lancelot. Could it really be true?

"Do you have proof of this story?" asked King Arthur.

"Yes!" And Whiskers showed them the very small gold scales from the dragon. "These were also a gift."

"A dragon!" Sir Lancelot exclaimed. "Did you fulfill your quest? Did you defeat him?"

"No," Prickles said in a very small voice. "He was already defeated. I felt sorry for him."

"Prickles sewed him up again with his sword," Whiskers said. "Just like he used his little quills to brush me. Hedgehogs are really very handy little things!"

At this, all the knights started to laugh. Prickles was so embarrassed, he didn't notice that King Arthur and Sir Lancelot weren't laughing at all. Instead, they looked at him with a growing respect.

Finally, King Arthur put a stop to the laughter and said, "It is time we heard from Sir Wyeth. Step forward, and declare yourself."

From the back of the hall came Sir Wyeth. He was very, very angry, and he seemed even larger than before, but there was something different about him. He wasn't smelly anymore, he was clean!

"Sire," he said, "this story is ridiculous. I am your own knight. You know I could never do these terrible things. Why would you listen to a silly little hedgehog? How could you believe this cat's lies? I've never seen him before in my life."

Whiskers was spitting, now, he was so mad. "You may not recognize me, now that I'm clean. You're clean too, somehow, but I still know you, and I'm ashamed to call you my master. From this moment I am free!"

And with that he flicked his tail at Sir Wyeth, sending loose bits of fur his way. Sir Wyeth started to sneeze, and sneeze, and with one last mighty sneeze, his jacket fell open and dropped soap and perfume all over the ground.

"So!" Lancelot said. "This is what you and your brothers were up to. Milk to make soap, and gold to buy perfume. Didn't you know the king would have given you soap and perfume if only you had asked?"

"Where are your brothers?" asked Sir Galahad.

"Find them!" cried Sir Gawaine.

Whiskers ran around the hall, flicking his tail at everyone, and soon found three more, very large, very clean men who were all sneezing just like their brother.

King Arthur said to Sir Wyeth, "You may smell of soap and perfume, but you are not pure of heart. You are a knave, and no true knight. Begone from here!"

And Sir Wyeth and his brothers ran from the hall, sneezing all the way home.

King Arthur said, "Whiskers, you have been a good friend to Prickles, and a great help to me. How can I thank you? Would you also like to go on a quest?"

"No, thank you, your Majesty. I would like to go back to the dairy, and live with the milkmaid. She was kind to me. But please sire, I beg you to give my friend Prickles another chance. He wants so much to be a knight."

Lancelot said, "I would be proud, sire, to have the hedgehog as my companion, and to fight at his side."

"Thank you Whiskers, thank you Lancelot," Prickles sniffled. "But I could not fulfill my quest. I am only a hedgehog, and I'm too small to be a knight."

"But, Prickles," said the king, smiling, "you already are a knight. Courage comes in all sizes, and you really do have a pure heart. You are a loyal friend, honest and brave and true. Kneel now, and pledge yourself to me."

Prickles climbed up the Round Table again, and knelt before the king on his tiny little claws. King Arthur picked up his fork, and very gently tapped it on each of the little creature's shoulders.

"I dub thee Sir Prickles, Hog of the Hedge."

As he rose once more, Prickles heard a noise, a wonderful, happy noise. And he knew exactly what it was.

"Hip Hip Hooray!" the crowd cheered. They were led by his two new best friends, Whiskers the cat and Sir Lancelot.

"Hip Hip Hooray! Hooray for Sir Prickles, the bravest of us all! Hooray for Sir Prickles, the Hedgehog Knight!"

The End